W9-CKZ-933

YOUR FUTURE IS
BRIGHT

Corey Finkle   Illustrated by Shelley Couvillion

Henry Holt and Company

New York

Henry Holt and Company, *Publishers since 1866*
Henry Holt® is a registered trademark of Macmillan Publishing Group, LLC.
120 Broadway, New York, NY 10271 ♦ mackids.com

Text copyright © 2021 by Corey Finkle
Illustrations copyright © 2021 by Shelley Couvillion
All rights reserved

Library of Congress Cataloging-in-Publication Data is available.
ISBN 978-1-250-62144-3

Our books may be purchased in bulk for promotional, educational, or business use.
Please contact your local bookseller or the Macmillan Corporate and Premium Sales Department at
(800) 221-7945 ext. 5442 or by email at MacmillanSpecialMarkets@macmillan.com.

First edition, 2021 / Design by Liz Dresner
The artist used watercolor, colored pencil, gouache, and digital to create the illustrations in this book.
Printed in China by RR Donnelley Asia Printing Solutions Ltd., Dongguan City, Guangdong Province

1 3 5 7 9 10 8 6 4 2

To Jill, Leo, and Sally,
for making my present, and future, so bright

—C. F.

To Coraline,
whatever your path, your future
will always be bright to me.

—S. C.

Today is a triumph. It's awesome! You're great!
The things you've accomplished are truly first-rate.
Your efforts have made you stand out from the crowd,
So puff out your chest; you deserve to feel proud.

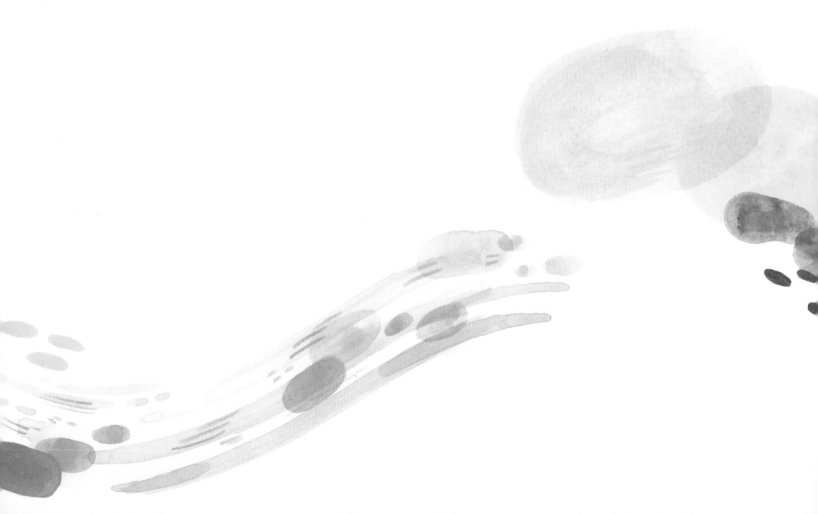

Amazing adventures are coming to you,
And people are eager to see what you'll do.

Your future is waiting. Which path will you choose?

There's no way to know . . .

but there are a few clues.

As soon as **you** get out of bed every day,
You're bursting with energy, ready to play.

You run at full speed as you zip place to place,
A grin of delight plastered over your face.

So maybe tomorrow we'll get to behold
Your fearless attempt as you race for the gold.

Or maybe you'll earn adoration and fame

In basketball,

soccer,

or some other game.

But while there's a chance you'll
be known for your feet,
The list of your options is *far*
from complete.

Your eyes and your ears are incredibly strong.
(No secret can ever stay hidden for long.)

So maybe you'll be a **detective**
or **spy**,
Discovering secrets as people
walk by.

And then there's **your** very refined sense of taste.
It'd be such a shame if that skill went to waste.

You could be a **baker** devising new sweets
To serve in a diner where everyone eats.

You have an artistic and passionate soul,
And that could be how you discover your role.

You might **write a novel**
that's loved and adored,

Or **star in a movie**
that wins an award.

You might paint a masterpiece, stunning and grand,

Or **play lead guitar** in a rock and roll band!

You're saddened whenever a classmate gets hurt.
If someone were freezing, you'd give them your shirt.

Perhaps you'll find happiness taking the lead,
Committing yourself to **help people in need.**

If **YOU** see injustice you don't kid around.

You fight for what's right until answers are found.

Tomorrow, you might offer voters a choice
To opt for a **leader** who gives them a voice.

This may be what happens, but then, maybe not.
Your interests might alter—it happens a lot.

Professor,

biologist,

architect,

nurse,

Astronomer probing the whole universe.

Accountant,

mechanic,

librarian,

vet,

Or something that nobody's thought to do yet!

Whatever you choose,
it will always seem smart,
As long as you follow
your generous heart.

When someone needs kindness, you answer the call,
And this tells us maybe the best news of all.

No matter what path you select in the end,

You'll always be known as a wonderful friend.

Don't ever stop dreaming, and set your sights high!

Tomorrow will come in the blink of an eye.

So follow your instincts to do what feels right . . .

... And you can be sure that your **future** is **bright**.